A BIG QUIET HOUSE

A YIDDISH FOLKTALE FROM EASTERN EUROPE

AUGUST HOUSE
Little Folk

RETOLD BY HEATHER FOREST
ILLUSTRATED BY SUSAN GREENSTEIN

Published 1996 by August House LittleFolk
augusthouse.com

Book Design by Harvill Ross Studios, Ltd., Little Rock, Ark.

Printed by Pacom Korea
Seoul, South Korea
November 2012

10 9 8 7 6 5 4 3   PB

LIBRARY OF CONGRESS CATALOGING-IN-PUBLICATION DATA

Forest, Heather.
A big quiet house : a Yiddish folktale from Eastern Europe / Heather Forest ;
illustrated by Susan Greenstein.
 p. cm.
Summary: Unable to stand his overcrowded and noisy home any longer, a man
goes to the wise old woman who lives nearby for advice.

ISBN 978-0-87483-604-2 (pb)
[1. Jews—Folklore. 2. Folklore—Europe, Eastern.]
I. Greenstein, Susan, ill.   II. Title.
PZ8.2'089924—dc20   1996
[E]   95-53739

First Hardcover Edition, 1996
First Paperback Edition,2000

The paper used in this publication meets the minimum requirements of the American National Standard
for Information Sciences— Permanence of Paper for Printed Library Materials, ANSI.48-1984

For my Grandmother Sadie and
my Grandfather Nathan
—H.F.

To my husband Phil and
my daughter Gina.
—S.G.

There once was a man whose house was very small.
It was cluttered with things from wall to wall.
Every day he would say, in a miserable way,
"I need more room."

One night, he tossed and turned in his bed. His wife's snoring and his children's giggling annoyed him. He covered his ears and grumbled, "There is too much noise! If I had a big quiet house I'd be able to sleep!"

As he lay awake, he thought about the wise old woman who lived at the edge of the village. "Perhaps *she* can solve my problem," he muttered. He threw off his covers, jumped out of bed, and went to seek the wise old woman.

He knocked impatiently at her door. She slowly opened it and said,
"It's the middle of the night! Why are you here?"

"I can't sleep," complained the man.
"My wife snores the whole night through.
My children annoy me by giggling, too.
What is a tired man to do?
Can you possibly solve my problem?
I need a big quiet house!"

The old woman scratched her head.
She considered a moment and then she said,
"Solve your problem? Yes, I can.
But first I must think of a plan."

Her face spread with a smile. "Go home and bring a big red chicken
in the house with you," she suggested.

"A CHICKEN?" asked the man, a bit bewildered.

But he went home and did as she told him to do.
She was the wisest woman he knew.

He caught his big, red, squawking chicken. He brought her into the
kitchen and let her go. The chicken strutted under the table.

"How is a chicken going to make my house bigger?" he wondered.

He went to his room, climbed into his bed, pulled the covers to his chin, and tried to fall asleep.

Meanwhile, the big red chicken crept out from under the table, wandered into the children's room, and began noisily pecking the son and daughter.

"B'bok! B'bok! B'bok!"

The wife tumbled with a *thump* onto the floor and chased the chicken.

Feathers were flying,
the children were crying,
the wife was sighing,
and the man couldn't sleep.

He threw off his covers, jumped out of bed, and went to the wise
old woman's house.

He knocked impatiently at her door. She opened it and said,
"It's the middle of the night! Go to sleep!"

"That's impossible!" he moaned. "I brought a big, red, noisy chicken
in the house with me.
Feathers are flying,
my children are crying,
my wife is sighing,
and I can't sleep!
Can you solve my problem?
I need a big quiet house!"

The old woman said, "Solve your problem? Yes, I can. I just didn't tell you the *whole* plan." She considered a moment and suggested, "Now, go home and bring a goat, a horse, a cow, and a sheep in the house with you."

"A GOAT, A HORSE, A COW, AND A SHEEP?" the man exclaimed.

But he went home and did as she told him to do.
She was the wisest woman he knew.

He herded a goat, a horse, a cow, and a sheep into his house.

Then, climbing clumsily over the animals, he got into his bed,
pulled the covers to his chin, and tried to fall asleep.

The sheep began to loudly sing, "Baaaaaaaaa!"

The goat chimed in with a lively "Maaaaaaaaa!"

The cow joined in with a melodious "Mooooooooo!"

The horse snorted and grandly sang, too: "Neigh,
neigh,
neigh!"

The singing and snorting woke the big red chicken, who wandered into the children's room and began noisily pecking the son and daughter.

"B'bok! B'bok! B'bok!"

The wife tumbled with a *thump* onto the floor and chased
the chicken.

Feathers were flying,
the children were crying,
the wife was sighing,
and the man couldn't sleep.

He threw off his covers, jumped out of bed, climbed over the animals, and went to the wise old woman's house.

He knocked loudly on her door. She opened it and yawned, "It's the middle of the night! You should be asleep!"

"That's impossible!" the man shouted. "How can I sleep with a chicken, a goat, a horse, a cow, and a sheep?
There is no room to walk in my house anymore.
Animals are everywhere from wall to door!
It is even noisier than before!
Feathers are flying,
my children are crying,
my wife is sighing,
and I can't sleep!
You said you could solve my problem!
I need a big quiet house!"

The old woman replied,
"Solve your problem? Yes, I can!
I just didn't tell you the *whole* plan.
Now, put all the animals back where they belong."

"Good idea!" exclaimed the man.

He went home, gathered the animals, and herded them all
into the barn.

Then he returned to his house and opened the door.

To his amazement, his house was not *small* anymore! He stared with wonder at the rooms. Now that all the animals were gone, his house seemed so empty, it looked remarkably *bigger*!

He climbed into his bed and pulled the covers up to his chin. Without the singing and snorting of the animals in the next room, his house was so *quiet*, he could hear the gentle snoring of his dear wife beside him. He heard his children giggling, too.

These ordinary sounds were no longer noise. They were music to his ears.

He smiled and thought, "What a big quiet house!
Next time I moan the whole day long,
complaining about what is going wrong,
I will stop and count my blessings first.
You know . . . It could always be worse."

And with a sigh he fell asleep.

ABOUT THE STORY

A BIG QUIET HOUSE is based on a popular Yiddish folktale and takes place in a *shtetl*, or a Jewish town in Eastern Europe. During the 18th, 19th, and 20th centuries, Jewish communities thrived in a geographical region bordered by Poland on the west, Russia on the east, Latvia on the north, and Rumania on the south. Although Eastern European Jews often spoke local languages to those who lived in the countryside around the Jewish ghettos, it was the Yiddish language which united the diverse Jewish population as a *mame-loshn*, or "mother tongue." While Hebrew was the language of prayer, Yiddish—an eclectic mixture of German, Polish, Russian, and Hebrew—was the language of conversation, witty expressions, and storytelling.

Jewish people of this era maintained a strong cultural identity despite constant persecution. The *shtetl* communities were destroyed by the ravages of World War II, yet the Yiddish culture of this region has been preserved in the folklore carried by emigrants throughout the world. At home, as a child, I delighted in hearing my older relatives, who immigrated to the United States from Eastern Europe, sprinkle their conversation with Yiddish expressions both comical and wise.

"A Big Quiet House" features a wise advisor who inspires a distressed man to view his personal problem with some relativity. Looking at small problems in the light of all troubles somehow diminishes the discomfort. A wry, comical example of Talmudic reasoning, this tale reflects the hopeful and philosophical approach to difficulties which has helped to sustain the Jewish culture throughout its long history.

Everyone has problems of one sort or another. Creative solutions can emerge by simply looking at difficulties from a new point of view. The unhappy man in this zany tale comes to realize, through personal experience, that his small problem, when compared to a larger one, vanishes entirely.

Attitude can dramatically affect perception. The size and peacefulness of the house in this Yiddish folktale do not really change. It is the man who changes, and the world he perceives is transformed.

My version of this farcical yet thought-provoking folktale is based on a variant entitled "It Could Always be Worse," found in *A Treasury of Jewish Folklore*, edited by Nathan Ausubel (New York: Crown Publishers, 1948).

—H.F.